Potato Joe

Keith Baker

Harcourt, Inc.

Orlando   Austin   New York   San Diego   London

Copyright © 2008 by Keith Baker

Requests for permission to make copies of any part of the work should be submitted online at www.harcourt.com/contact or mailed to the following address: Permissions Department, Harcourt, Inc., 6277 Sea Harbor Drive, Orlando, Florida 32887-6777.

www.HarcourtBooks.com

Library of Congress Cataloging-in-Publication Data
Baker, Keith, 1953—
Potato Joe/Keith Baker.
p.   cm.
Summary: Joe finds all sorts of uses for the potatoes in the familiar nursery rhyme,
"One Potato, Two Potato."
1. Nursery rhymes, American.   2. Children's poetry, American.
[1. Nursery rhymes.   2. Counting-out rhymes.]   I. Title.
PZ8.3.B175Pot   2008
811'.54—dc22   2007005930
ISBN 978-0-15-206230-9

First edition
A C E G H F D B

Manufactured in China

The illustrations in this book were done in Adobe Photoshop.
The display lettering was created by Keith Baker.
The text type was set in Kabel.
Color separations by Bright Arts Ltd., Hong Kong
Manufactured by South China Printing Company, Ltd., China
Production supervision by Christine Witnik
Designed by Keith Baker

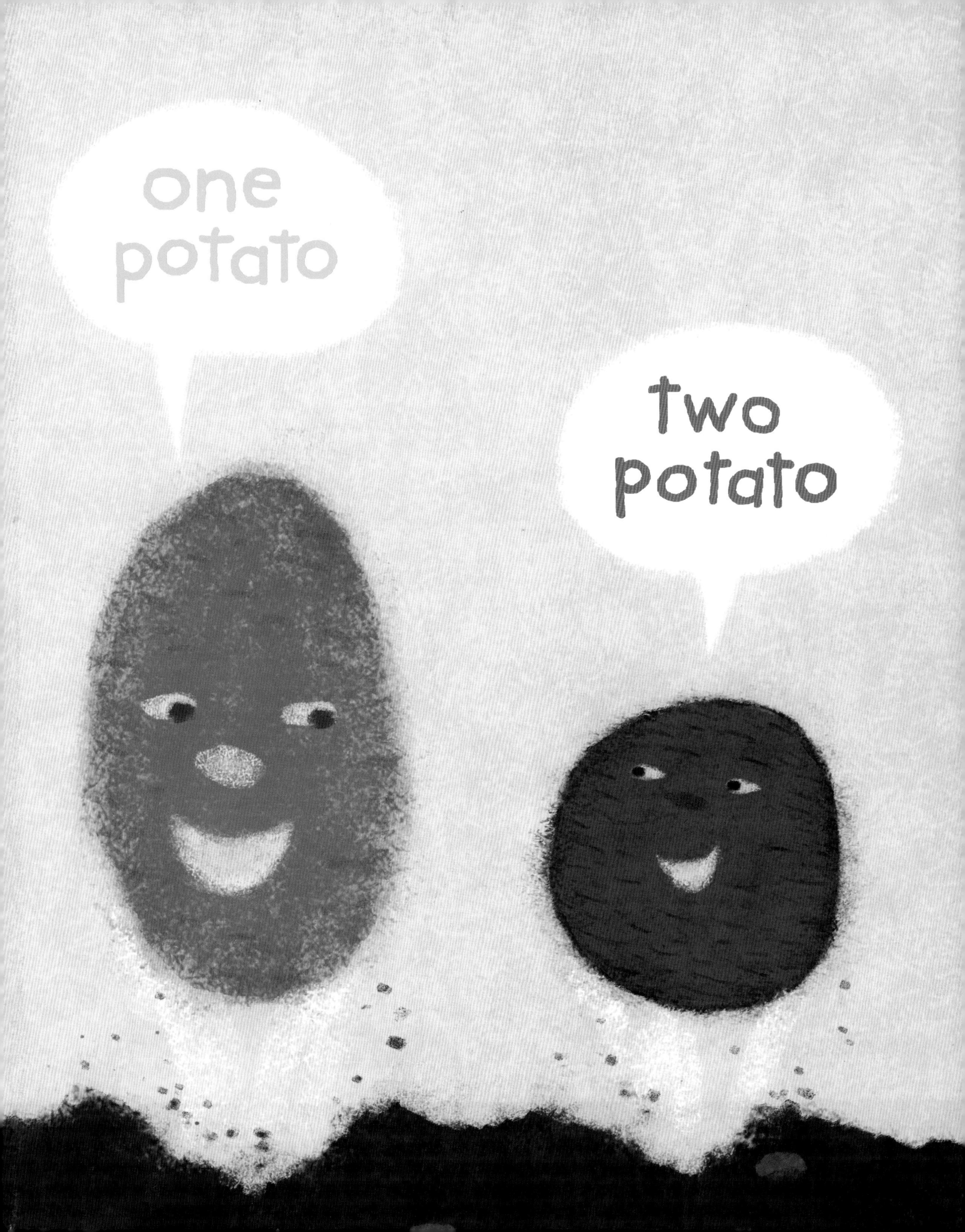
one potato
two potato

hello, Joe!

three
potato

four
potato

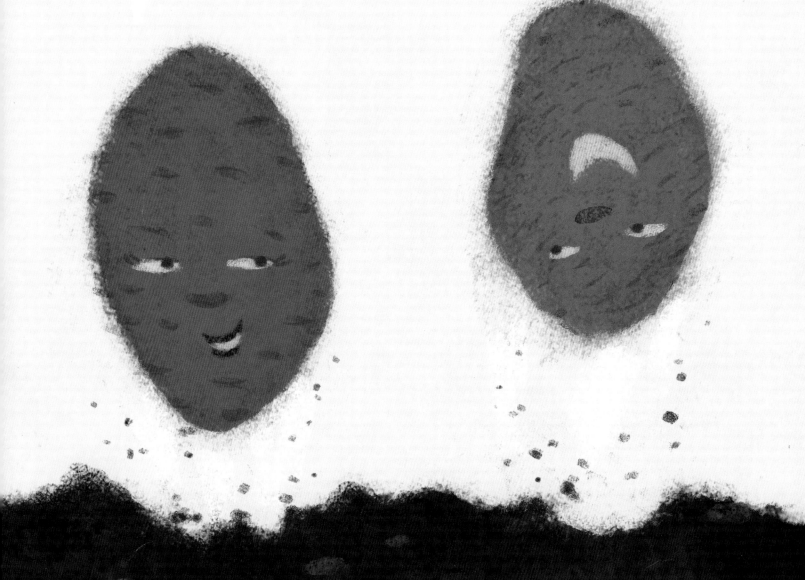

tic-
tac-
toe!

five
potato

six
potato

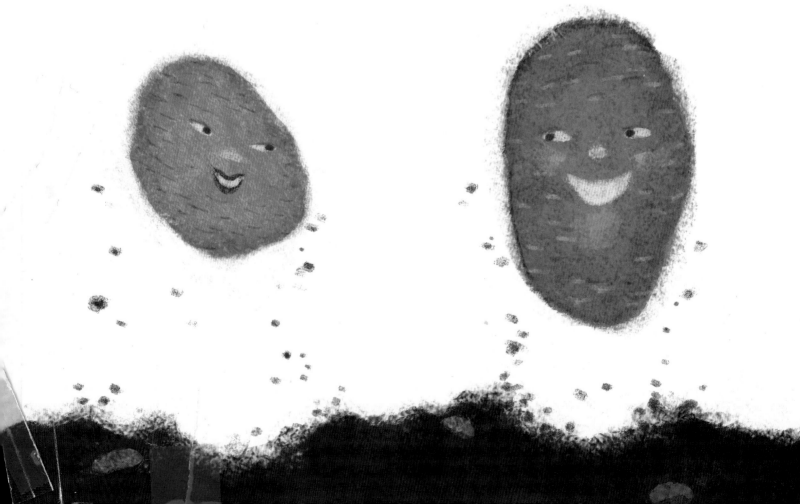

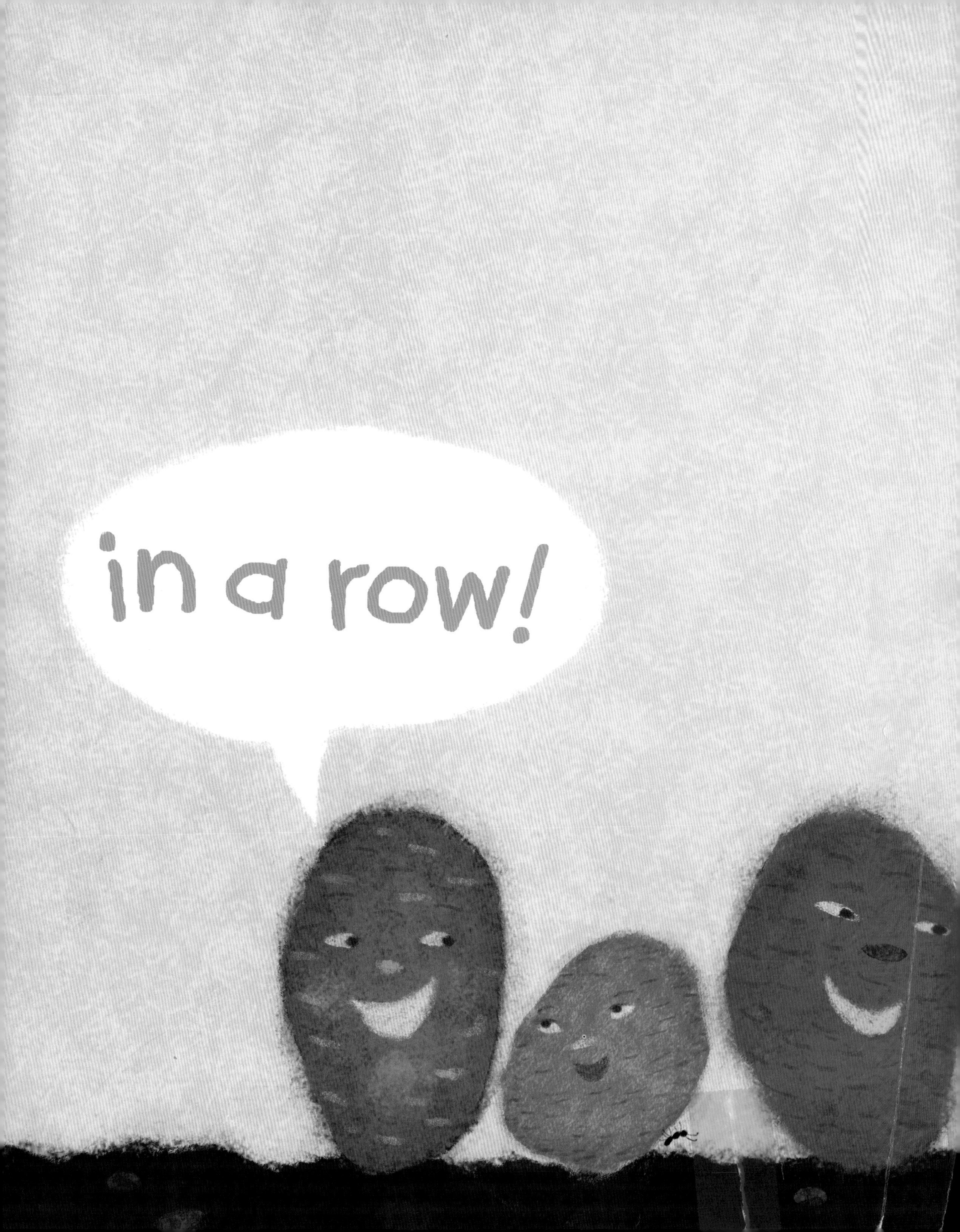
in a row!

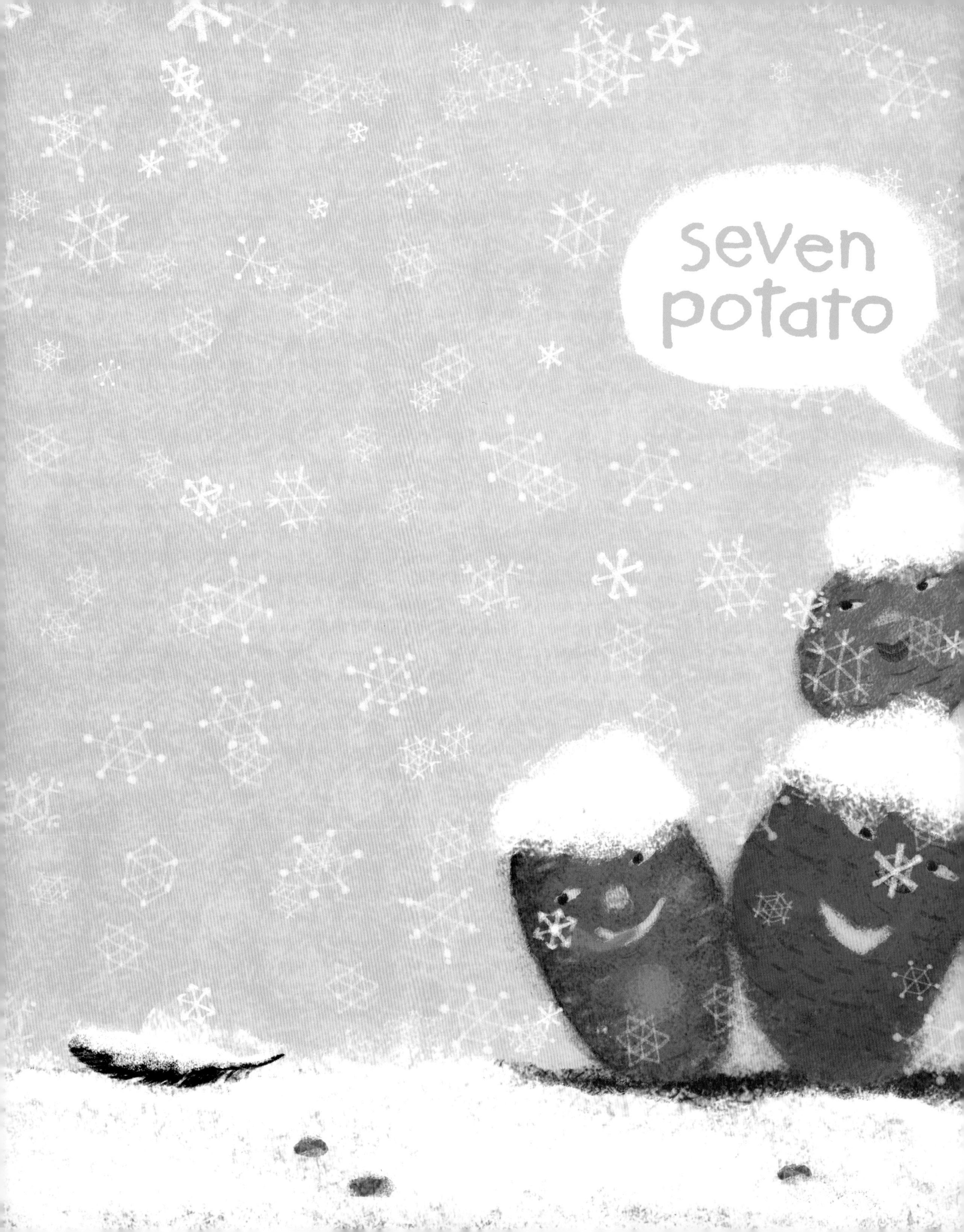
seven
potato

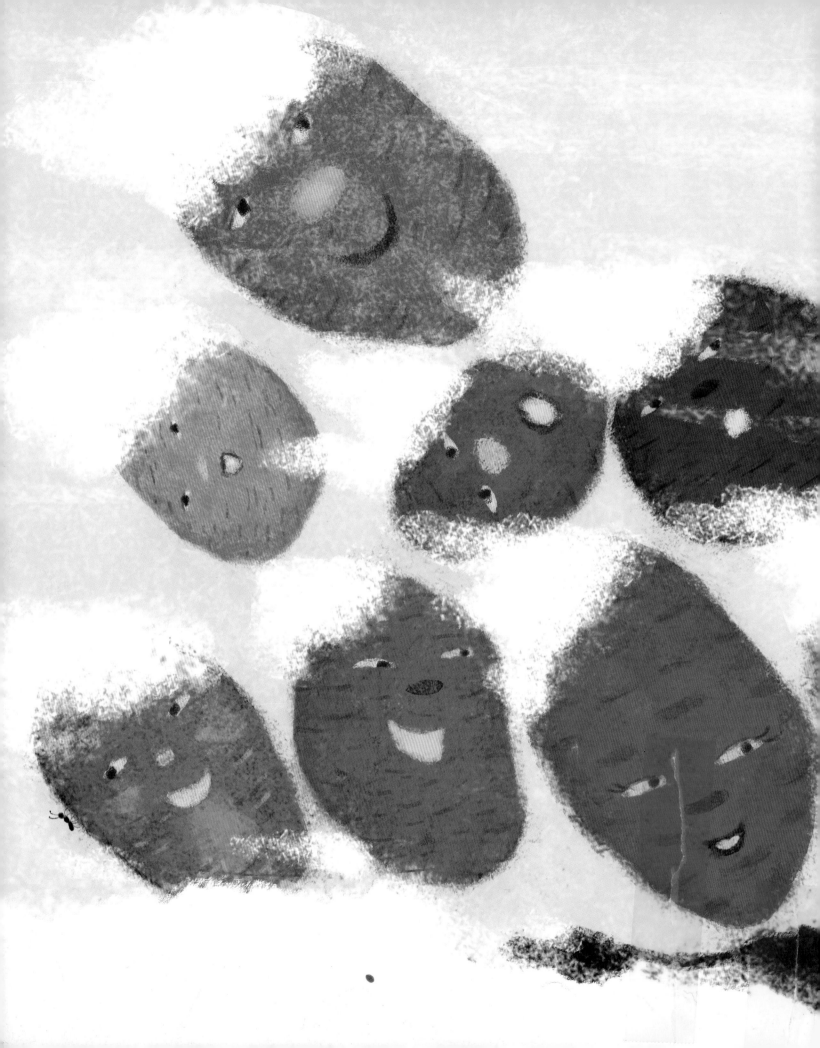

swing your
partner

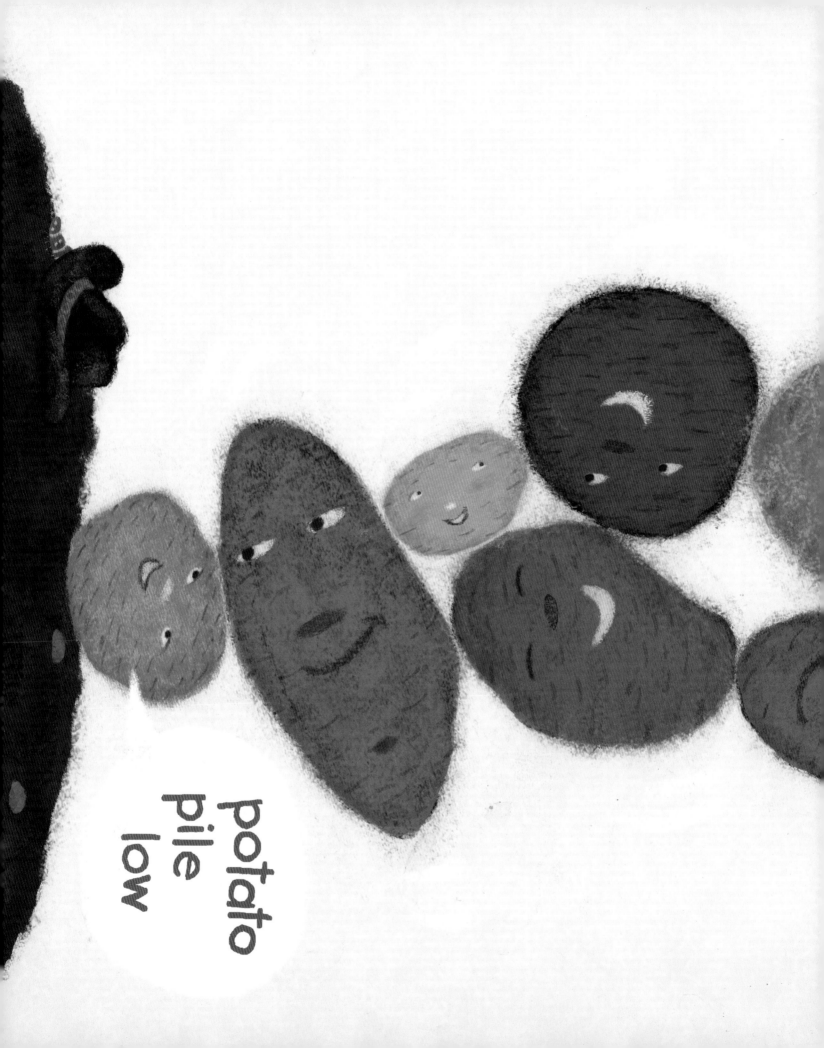

potato
pile
low

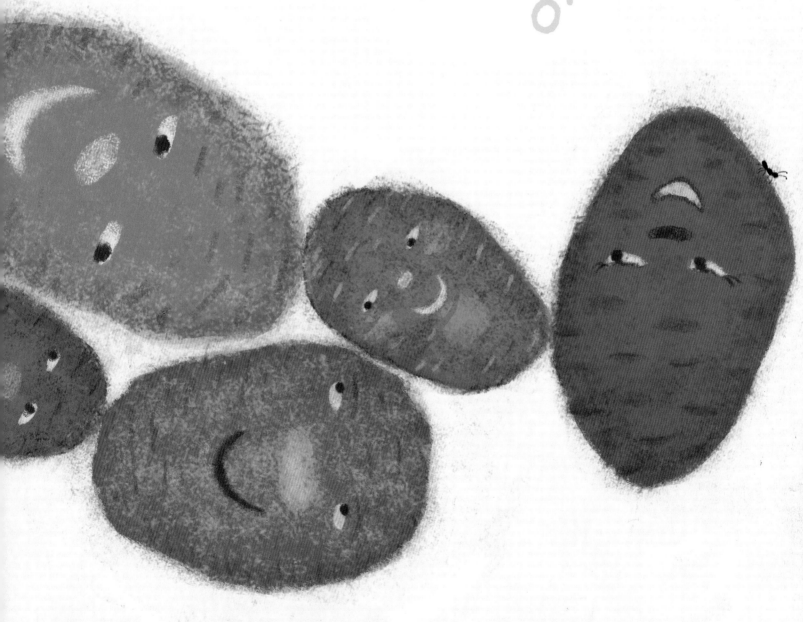

potato
pile
high

roll on over,
Tomato Flo!

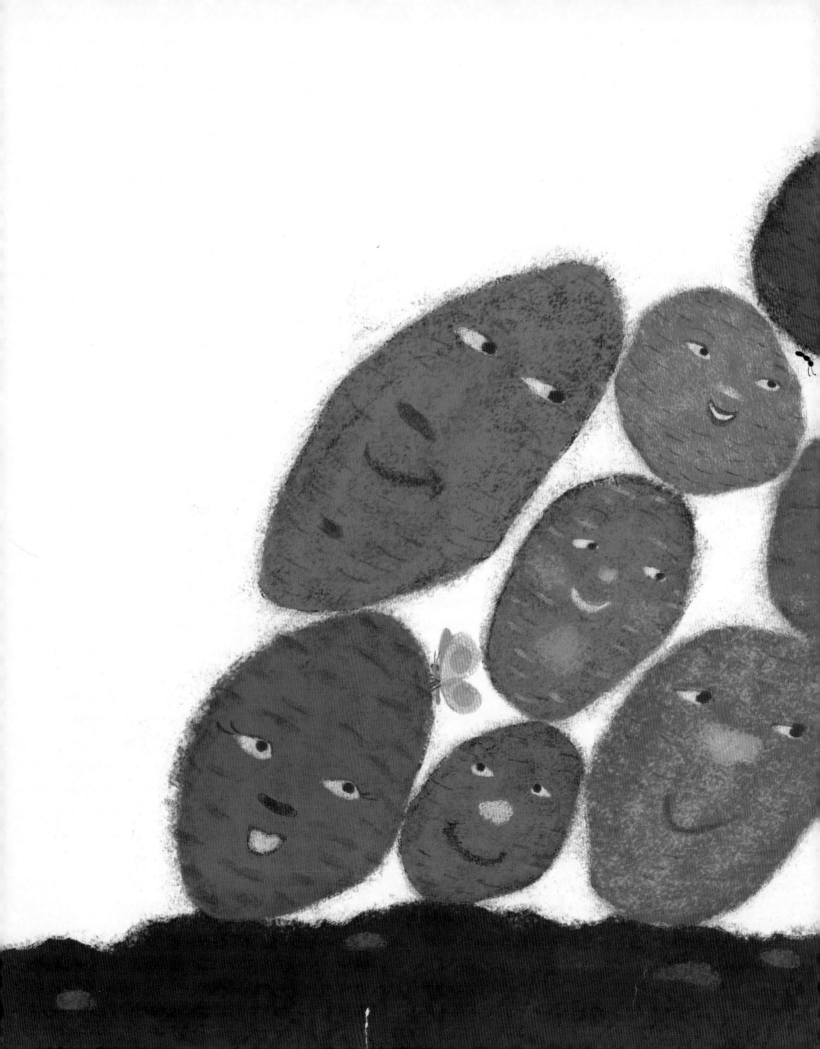

now
back to the
garden—
everybody
roll!

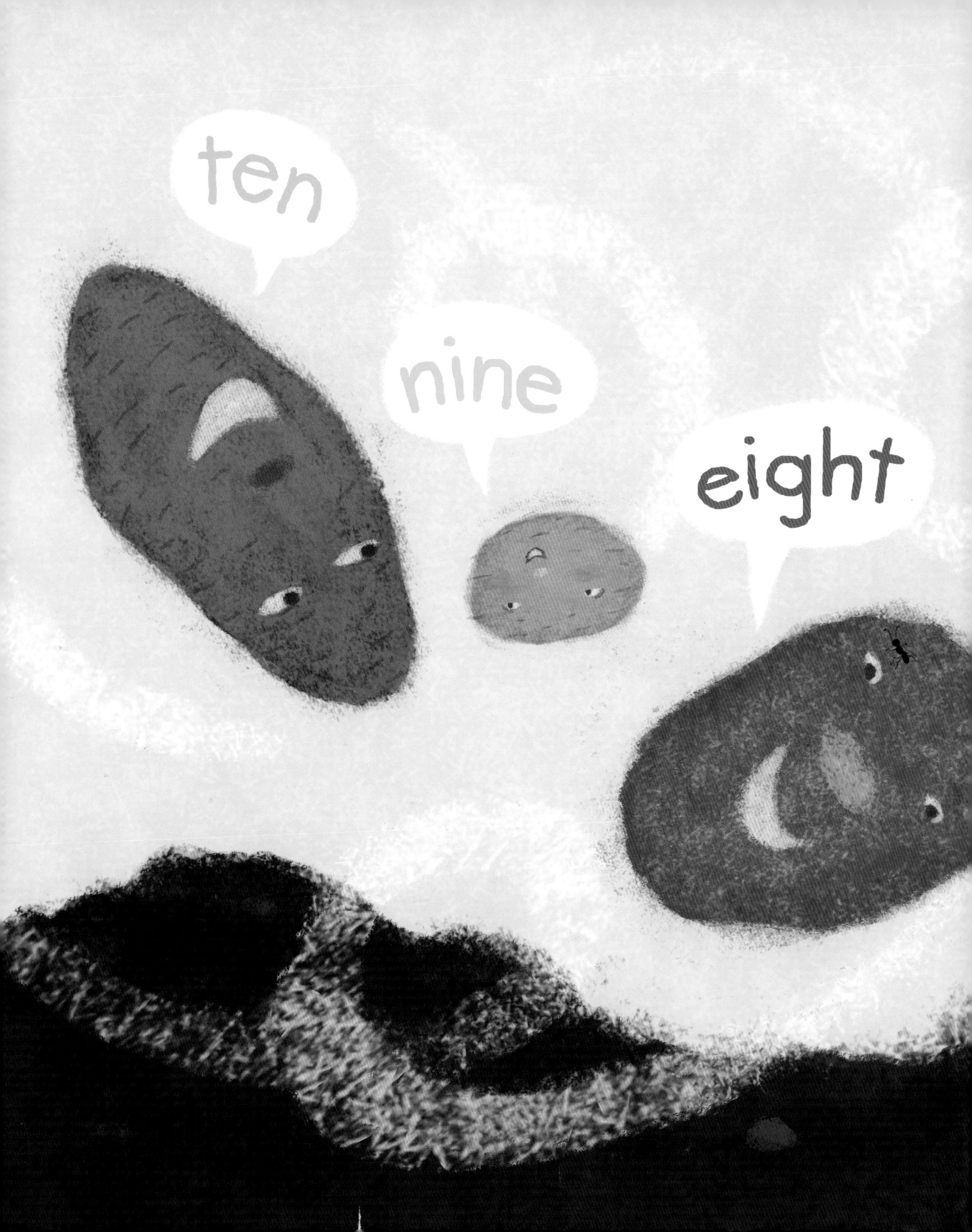
ten
nine
eight

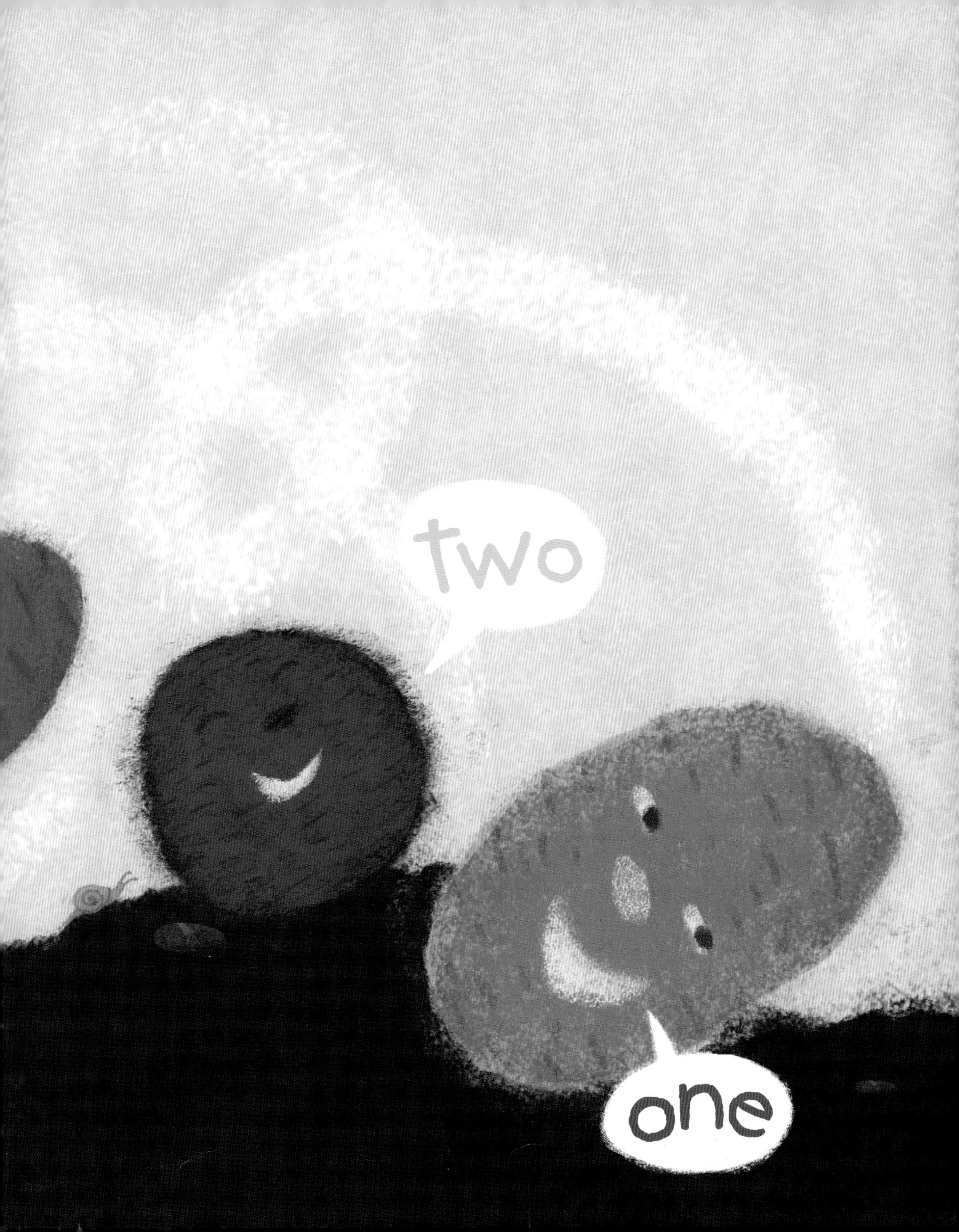
two
one

Potato Joe!

down in
the dirt—

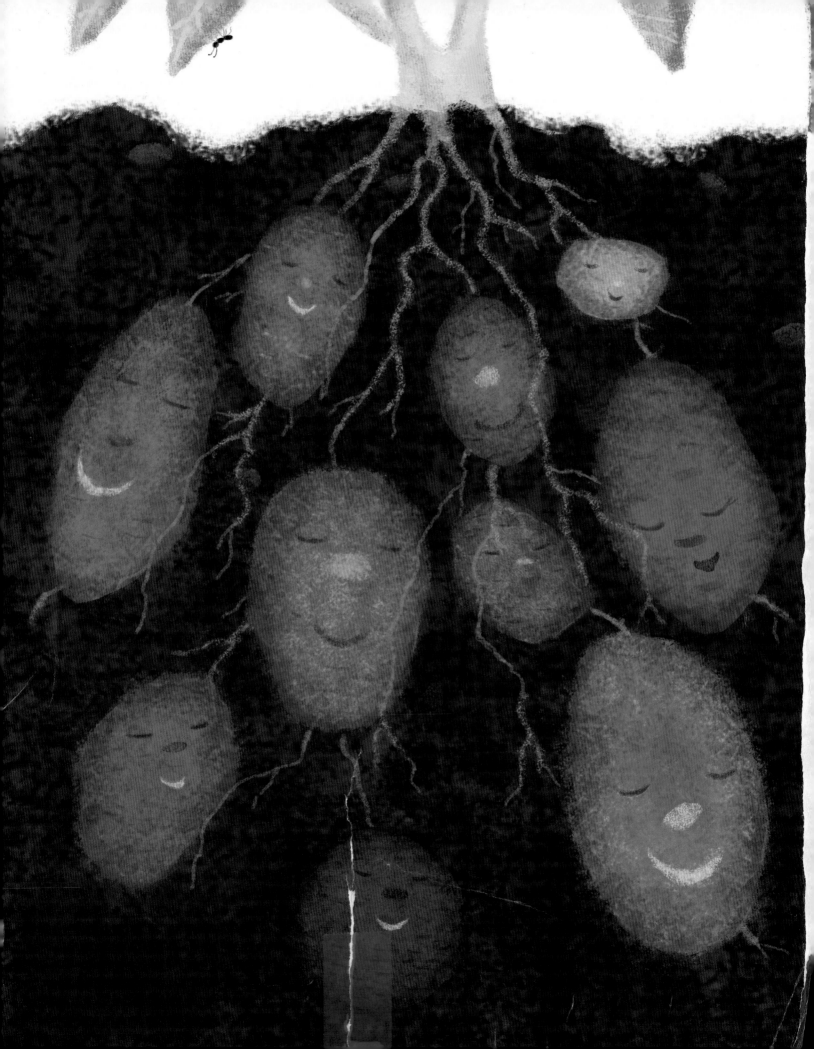